Myths and Legends of the Desert

By John Malam

KINGFISHER

THE NILE – SOURCE OF LIFE

Over 5,000 years ago, the great civilization of ancient Egypt grew up on the banks of the river Nile. Here, in the usually barren desert, the land was very fertile. Every summer the river Nile flooded, washing wet, black soil onto the land nearby. When the flood waters went down, farmers planted crops to feed the people and animals and, as a result, a civilization developed there. The yearly floods were so important that the Egyptians called their land *Kemet* 'the black land', after the mud that so vital to their life and prosperity.

MEDITERRANEAN SEA

LOWER EGYPT

GIZA ●   ● CAIRO

UPPER EGYPT

RED SEA

THEBES ●

ABU SIMBEL ●

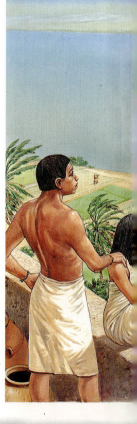

The river Nile flows north through Egypt towards the Mediterranean Sea. The ancient Egyptians lived on the river's flood plain, a narrow strip of fertile land, marked in green on the map. It measured between 2 and 40 km wide.

The ancient Egyptians believed in many gods. Each god looked after something important in daily life. The god of the flood was called Hapy. He was shown with a headdress made of river plants. His plump features reminded people how much they depended on the Nile's annual flood for their food.

FLOODS OF TEARS

The ancient Egyptians made up stories about their gods. They were used to explain things that were important to people in their everyday lives. To explain the annual flooding of the Nile, they told how the god Osiris, who taught the people how

to farm and worship the gods, was murdered by his jealous brother, Seth. On hearing this news, the goddess Isis, who was both his wife and sister, began to cry. Her tears fell like rain into the Nile. It was said that Isis cried so much her tears caused the river to flood.

WHEN TIME BEGAN

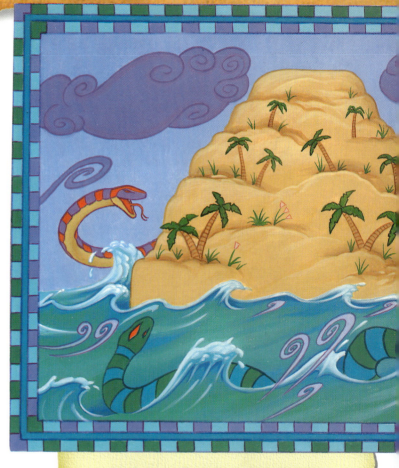

The ancient Egyptians were curious about how the world had been created. Like many other ancient peoples the Egyptians devised creation stories to explain how the world had come into existence. They had lots of ideas, mostly formed around their different gods.

According to one creation myth, the world had been created by the god Ptah. Egyptian artists showed him as a mummy with green skin – the colour of plant life and rebirth. It was said he created the world by thought alone, then made everything in it simply by speaking their names.

HOW THE WORLD WAS CREATED

Another creation myth begins with a time before heaven and earth existed. The only thing in the universe was an ocean of chaos. It was a shapeless ocean that went on forever without end. The people of Egypt said that this ocean was a god, who they called Nun. One day, a mound of dry soil rose slowly out of the waters of Nun. This first land they called the 'primeval mound' and it was Egypt.

The ancient Egyptians believed that Nun was the god of infinity and chaos. They thought he had always existed and would continue to do so, no matter what happened. People feared that one day Nun would return to send the world back into the ocean of chaos. To the ancient Egyptians Nun was also the god of never-ending darkness. They believed that each night it was Nun who carried the sun-god away, taking him through the darkness of the underworld.

Some people think that pyramids may have been shaped the way they are to make them look like the primeval mound.

BIRTH OF THE SUN GOD

The sun played a major part in the lives of the ancient Egyptians. It was both a creator and a destroyer. Its heat and light helped crops to grow and ripen, which fed the people, but it could also destroy the land by drying fields until they turned into barren desert. Because of this power, the sun was worshipped as a god and related things were held sacred.

The ancient Egyptians built huge needle-like obelisks as monuments to the sun-god Ra. It was said that when the primeval mound rose out of the waters of Nun, the legendary benu-bird landed on the mound. The Egyptians believed that the benu-bird was Ra in disguise.

The scarab beetle was sacred to the ancient Egyptians. They saw how it rolled balls of animal dung along the ground and they linked this with the god Khepri, who people believed was responsible for rolling the sun across the sky each day.

The sun-god Ra was king of the gods. Artists showed him as a human figure with the head of a hawk, wearing a sun-shaped headdress.

Because Khepri was responsible for the appearance of the sun every morning, the scarab beetle was linked with eternal life. The ancient Egyptians carried amulets and wore rings in the shape of the scarab, and mummies were buried with winged scarabs. Even the evil Imhotep in the film The Mummy Returns believed that scarabs could protect him.

The lotus flower, a species of water lily, grew at the edge of the river Nile. Its large flowers opened at dawn with the rising of the new day's sun. The ancient Egyptians believed it represented the sun's rebirth, bringing light and heat into the world, and banishing darkness.

THE BIRTH OF RA, BRINGER OF LIGHT AND HEAT

According to legend, a blue lotus flower mysteriously appeared one day out of the dark waters of Nun. As the flower opened its petals, it revealed a beautiful child who was Ra. Having created himself by magic, Ra then created the world and everything in it.

During the twelve hours of night he travelled through the endless blackness of the underworld. At dawn, he reappeared in the sky. For the next twelve hours he sailed across the sky in his solar barque (boat). He took this journey every day and made the Egyptians very happy.

SKY AND EARTH CREATED

The ancient Egyptians believed that everything in the world had an exact opposite. They saw how their world was divided into opposing parts – the fertile strip along the banks of the river Nile, and the barren, sandy desert beyond. This belief in opposites is found in many of their myths, as seen in this one about the sky and the earth.

NUT AND GEB

Nut and Geb were twins, who had loved each other from the beginning of time. They hugged so tightly that nothing could come between them, not even the sun's rays. This upset the sun-god Ra, who wanted to send his light and warmth into the world.

Ra ordered that Nut and Geb should be separated. Their father, Shu, the god of air, agreed to separate his children and to hold them apart. He forced his way between them and pushed upwards. Nut was raised into a high arch and became the sky. Far below her, Geb became the earth. By day, the twins were apart and Ra's sunlight reached the world. But as night fell, Nut came down to be with her brother. Nut clung to Geb through the darkness, until Shu forced her skywards again as a new day began.

THE FIRST PHARAOH

PHARAOH SAVES HUMANKIND

When the world was new, Ra ruled as the first pharaoh. Each day he sailed through the heavens in his solar barque, bringing light and heat to Egypt. As Ra grew older his strength began to fail and some people saw his weakness as an opportunity to take his place. But Ra was far wiser than they knew. He sent his daughter, the lion-goddess Sekhmet, to kill the rebels.

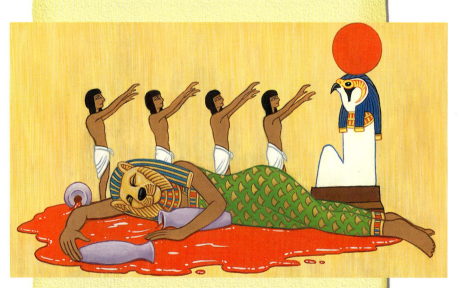

Sekhmet liked the taste of human blood so much that she carried on killing long after she had defeated the rebels. The human race was in danger of being destroyed and Ra saw that he had to stop his daughter. He ordered some beer to be coloured red so Sekhmet would think that it was blood. She drank it and became very drunk, completely losing her senses. Sekhmet was no longer a danger, and Ra had saved humankind.

Ra, the sun-god, was the first pharaoh, or king, of ancient Egypt. After Ra, the pharaohs were born as humans, but the day they became Egypt's new ruler, the people believed they were no longer mortal: they had become gods living among ordinary people. To them, the pharaoh was a god-king, with the same power as Ra and the other gods, who had come to do the gods' work on Earth.

People believed that Sekhmet protected the pharaoh and Egypt from harm by destroying his enemies with her fiery breath. She was shown as a woman with the head of a lion. Her name means 'she who is powerful'.

Beer was a common drink in ancient Egypt and beermaking was an important task. Even children drank beer as it was a nutritious part of the Egyptian diet. It was slightly alcoholic with a thick soupy consistency and was flavoured with honey, spices or herbs. Beer did not keep long so was drunk soon after being made.

The pharaoh had many titles, one of which was Son of Ra. It was considered rude to talk directly about a living god, so people referred to their king as Per-aa, meaning great house (the palace in which the king lived). Over the years the meaning of Per-aa changed, until by around 1350 BC it referred to the king himself. From Per-aa came the word pharaoh.

The civilization of ancient Egypt didn't just suddenly appear out of nowhere. Egyptian society developed over many centuries until it grew into a highly organized system, run by government officials throughout the land. However, the ancient Egyptians themselves believed their great civilization was a gift from the gods, in particular Osiris, god of rebirth and growth.

Osiris was also the god of the afterlife and the dead. He was usually shown as a mummy, dressed in white to represent the bandages used in mummification. To show he was a king, he held the crook and the flail, and wore the Atef Crown, which had ostrich feathers on it. His green face represented rebirth and growth.

It was believed that Osiris had taught the Egyptians how to lead civilized lives and how to grow all the food they needed – wheat, barley, grapes and other fruits. Before this, it was said that people were cannibals.

OSIRIS, BRINGER OF CIVILIZATION

When Nut, the goddess of the sky, wanted to have children the mighty sun-god Ra would not let her. He cursed Nut to prevent her from bearing children on any day of the year. At the time, a year had only 360 days, all created by Ra. The wise god Thoth took pity on Nut, and won five extra days of light from the moon. This made the year 365 days long. And, because Ra had no power over the new days, Nut was able to bear children on them.

On the first new day she bore a son, Osiris. At the moment of his birth a voice proclaimed: "A great and kind pharaoh is born." And this was true. Osiris became the pharaoh and taught the Egyptians about farming and religion. He brought civilization to the land of Egypt, and for that he was one of the best loved and most important gods of all.

The crook and the flail carried by Osiris were carried by all of Egypt's pharaohs. The crook was the shape of a shepherd's staff and symbolized government. It may be related to the idea of the pharoah as a shepherd leading his flock (his people). The flail was like a shepherd's fly-whisk and may have symbolized protection, representing the pharaoh's power to brush aside enemies and other dangers.

Crowns and headdresses were worn by the pharaoh to show his authority. The Double Crown combined the White Crown of Upper Egypt and the Red Crown of Lower Egypt, showing the pharaoh ruled all of Egypt.

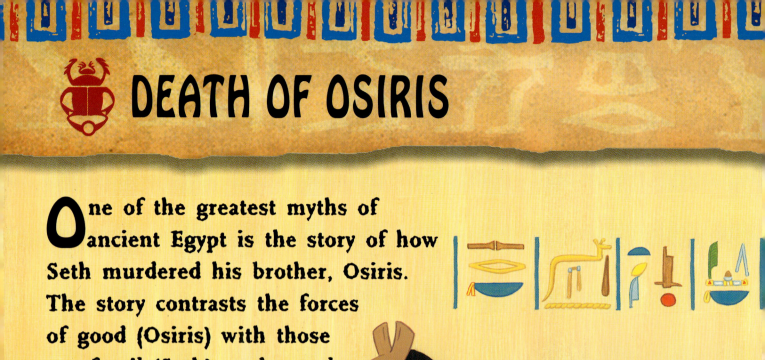

DEATH OF OSIRIS

One of the greatest myths of ancient Egypt is the story of how Seth murdered his brother, Osiris. The story contrasts the forces of good (Osiris) with those of evil (Seth), and reveals the ancient Egyptian's deep interest in life after death.

OSIRIS IS MURDERED

The sky goddess Nut gave birth to four more children after her beloved Osiris. Among them were Isis, the goddess of fertility and nature, and Seth, the god of chaos and evil. As Osiris grew in power he was much loved by the people of Egypt. Seth became so jealous of his brother he devised a cunning way to get rid of him. Seth ordered a beautiful box to be made, in the exact size of Osiris. He said he would give it to the man it fitted. When Osiris lay inside the box, it fitted him perfectly. Seth slammed the lid shut and threw the box into the river Nile.

Osiris drowned, and thus death was created. The box had become his coffin. Isis, who was both sister and wife to Osiris, went in search of his coffin. She found it in a faraway place and brought it home to Egypt. Isis hid the coffin in the marshes, but Seth found it one day when he was out hunting. Angered by the return of Osiris, Seth cut his brother's dead body into fourteen pieces and scattered them throughout the land.

To the ancient Egyptians, the day on which a person died was "the night of going forth to life". In other words, death was not the end, merely the beginning of something new, something wonderful. This strong belief in the afterlife can be seen in both the myths and legends of the ancient Egyptians and through the legacy they have left behind.

The ancient Egyptians not only built pyramids and tombs. Near the pharaoh Khafre's pyramid at Giza, they built the Great Sphinx, although no-one is completely sure why. The sphinx was a mythical beast with the body of a lion and the head of a man. The face is probably that of Khafre himself.

The ancient Egyptians built huge pyramids as tombs for the early pharaohs. They were massive structures built of stone or mud-brick. The people believed that they were building homes in which the spirits of the dead ruler would live, looking after him while he made the long journey to the afterlife. After around 1550 BC, pharaohs were buried in tombs cut into the sides of hills, not in pyramids.

ISIS FINDS THE BODY OF OSIRIS

Isis could not bear to be parted from Osiris, so she set out to bring him back to life by gathering up the pieces of his body that Seth had hidden throughout Egypt. She changed herself into a bird and flew far and wide looking for Osiris. Slowly, Isis collected the pieces, save one which Seth had thrown into the Nile and had been eaten by a great fish. Isis found the head of Osiris at the city of Abydos, and his heart at Athribis. In each place she held a funeral ceremony, hoping to trick Seth into thinking Osiris had been buried there. With all the pieces of Osiris's body together in one place, Isis felt sure the dead king could be made to live again. But all her powers of magic were not enough to perform that miracle. She broke down and cried.

Duamutef jar: stomach

Hapy jar: lungs

Qebehsenuef jar: intestines

Imsety jar: liver

The ancient Egyptians perfected the gruesome craft of preserving bodies, known as *mummification*. According to Egyptian mythology, the first mummy ever made was that of Osiris. He survived death, and went on to become the ruler of the afterlife, which was the Egyptian idea of heaven. It was the place everyone hoped to go to after they died. They thought of it as a beautiful fertile landscape, filled with sunshine and happiness.

Four containers, known as canopic jars, were used to hold the different organs of a mummified body. The jars represented the four Sons of Horus.

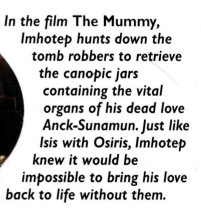

In the film **The Mummy**, Imhotep hunts down the tomb robbers to retrieve the canopic jars containing the vital organs of his dead love Anck-Sunamun. Just like Isis with Osiris, Imhotep knew it would be impossible to bring his love back to life without them.

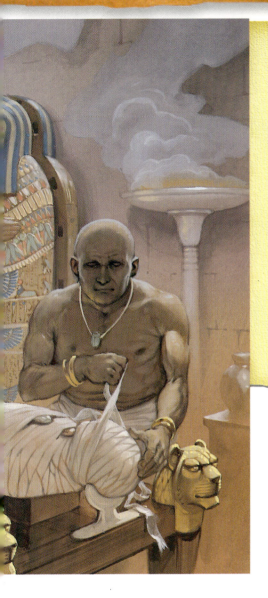

OSIRIS IS REBORN AND LIVES AGAIN

When Isis realized she could not bring Osiris back to life, she knelt beside his dead body and cried so hard that the mighty sun-god Ra heard her. Ra took pity on her and sent two gods to help – Anubis, the god of embalming and Thoth, the god of wisdom.

Anubis bathed each severed part of Osiris's body, then wrapped it in bandages. Isis and Thoth helped to place the pieces together in the shape of the king's body, and bandaged the body together. The first mummy had been made. Using her magic, Isis blew the breath of life into Osiris, but he did not want to come back into the world of the living. Instead, Osiris stayed in the underworld, the home of the dead, where he would live as their king for ever.

Amulets, the "lucky charms" designed to protect the wearer from danger and illness, were wrapped between the bandages of mummies. They were to protect the person on their journey to the afterlife.

A person's spirit had to pass tests on the journey to the afterlife. The most important was the Weighing of the Heart Ceremony, in which the person's heart was weighed against the feather of truth. A person who had lived a good life was allowed to go forth, but a bad person was not. Their heart was eaten by the crocodile-headed goddess Ammut, and the person never reached the afterlife.

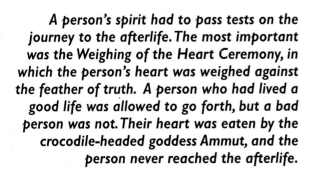

POISONOUS CREATURES

Like many good stories, the myths of the ancient Egyptians used magic and mystery to keep people interested in them. For extra excitement, storytellers added some frightening elements. Stories were especially scary when they involved real poisonous animals, such as scorpions and snakes, which people might come across in their everyday lives.

Two main types of scorpion live in Egypt – a pale-skinned poisonous variety, and a less harmful darker-skinned species.

A scorpion was the symbol of the goddess Selket. People believed she had the power to cure them of poisonous bites and stings.

In 1898, archaeologists in Egypt found part of a stone macehead, on which was a picture of a king. In front of him is the sign of a scorpion, so archaeologists called him King Scorpion. Very little is known about him except that he lived around 3100 BC and may have been one of Egypt's earliest pharaohs. This find led to the creation of the Scorpion King in the film The Mummy Returns.

ISIS AND THE SEVEN SCORPIONS

Unbeknownst to Seth, Osiris and Isis had a son, named Horus. Isis and Horus lived in the marshes, where they hoped to keep safe from Seth. But he found them and locked them up. They were saved by the god Thoth who sent seven magic scorpions to guide them back to the marshes. On the way, they asked a rich woman for shelter but, seeing the scorpions, she slammed her door in Isis's face. Although a poor woman gave them shelter, the scorpions were still angry about the rich woman's rudeness and decided to teach her a lesson.

They gave all their poison to their leader, Tefen, who crept into her house and stung her baby as he slept. Isis heard the woman's screams and went to help her. She took the baby in her arms and ordered the deadly poison to leave his body. The baby was saved, and the woman saw that the stranger she had sent away was the goddess Isis. Filled with remorse, she gave all her wealth to Isis and the poor woman who had shown such kindness to a stranger.

In **The Mummy Returns** *the Scorpion King is depicted as a fearsome warrior. As his army lies dying in the desert, following defeat in a huge battle, the Scorpion King makes a pact with Anubis. If he is helped to win one last war, his soul will belong to Anubis for all time.*

Horus became a popular god, like his father Osiris. Pharaohs called themselves *the Living Horus*, which was a way of saying they were the god himself, living among people. Horus represented many things to the ancient Egyptians, but nothing more so than the power to heal and protect. This belief arose from the final part of the myth, where he fought many battles with his uncle Seth for control of Egypt.

HOW HORUS BECAME PHARAOH

Isis and her baby son Horus returned to hide in the marshes. However, Seth changed into a poisonous snake and bit Horus. Isis called upon the sun-god Ra to help her. Using all his power, Ra cured Horus. Years passed, and Horus grew powerful. He became the king of Lower Egypt, and this made Seth jealous.

Seth and Horus fought over which of them should rule Egypt. At first, Seth was the stronger, and he cut out Horus's left eye. After 80 years of fighting, Horus and Seth were brought before the gods to settle the quarrel. Osiris threatened to unleash demons from the underworld if Horus, his son, was not made king of all Egypt. His threat worked and Horus was made pharaoh. As for Seth, he left the earth to live in the sky, where he became the god of storms.

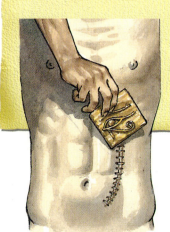

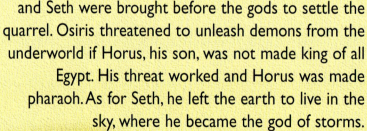

When embalmers had finished their work of preserving a body, a metal or wax plaque was often placed over the cut. On it was drawn the eye of Horus, designed to heal and protect the dead person in the afterlife.

Horus's restored eye was known as his wedjat-eye or healed-eye. The eye of Horus was a popular amulet (charm) worn by people as a healing symbol. They believed it would heal them if they became ill or injured.

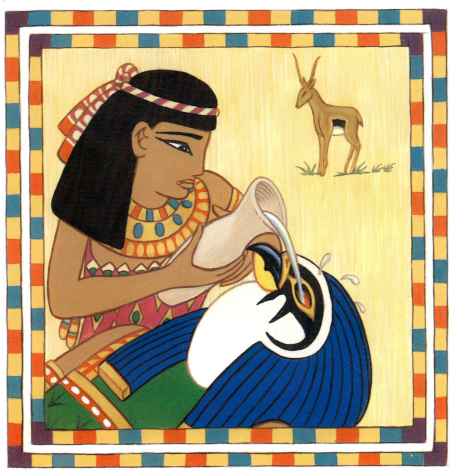

After Horus had his left eye cut out, the goddess Hathor found him crying in the desert. She caught a gazelle, milked it and poured the milk into Horus's empty eye socket. His sight was miraculously restored.

*Horus, whose name means **Distant One**, was portrayed by Egyptian artists as a man with the head of a hawk. The Double Crown shows he was the ruler of all Egypt.*

A DANGEROUS JOURNEY

The ancient Egyptians wanted to understand the world in which they lived. When they saw the sun setting in the west, disappearing below the horizon, they wondered where it went to and what happened to it during the night. As the sun set, it seemed to sink into the vast sandy desert to the west of Egypt. This made the Egyptians fear the desert, which they believed was the entrance to the underworld, a place where danger lurked.

RA FIGHTS APEP

As the sun set in the West, the sun-god Ra began his nightly journey through the dark and dangerous underworld. He took with him many other gods, including Thoth, Hathor and Seth. As Ra's light reached into the darkest, furthest parts of the underworld, the terrible demons that lived there stirred.

Chief among them was the great and fearful snake-god Apep. Each night, he attacked Ra, hoping to kill him and so prevent him from rising once more into the sky. Their fight lasted all night but as dawn approached, Ra cut off the snake's head. It was not enough to kill Apep, who slithered into the darkness where his wounds would heal. Ra was free to rise into the morning sky, bringing light and heat to the world. But each night, he would meet with Apep again, and they would fight once more.

THE BOOK OF THOTH

Most people in ancient Egypt could not read or write. Those who could belonged to a group of highly skilled workers known as scribes. Writing was linked with the gods. It was said that the god Thoth had brought writing to the land of Egypt. Stories were told about Thoth's wisdom and what happened to those who tried to steal his knowledge.

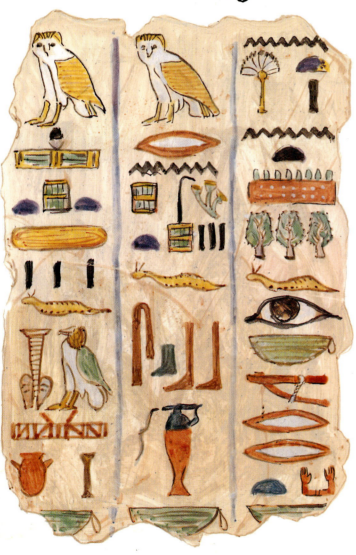

A scribe sat cross-legged on the ground. He pulled his kilt tight, making a flat surface. He wrote with a reed brush or pen, held in his right hand. He used his left hand to hold and unroll the papyrus on which he wrote.

The ancient Egyptians invented a type of writing that used some 700 different signs. These hieroglyphs were mainly used to write sacred texts. They could be written from left to right or right to left in rows, or in columns.

In the film The Mummy, Evy can decipher ancient Egyptian hieroglyphs. When she uses her knowledge to read aloud a spell written in hieroglyphs it unfortunately leads to trouble. Imhotep's mummy is brought back to life by the incantation.

Thoth was the god of wisdom, writing, reading and mathematics. Artists showed him as a human figure with the head of an ibis bird. In his hand he held a scribe's writing palette.

THE STORY OF PRINCE SETNA

There was nothing that Prince Setna could not read or write. One day, he read about Prince Neferkeptah who had lived long ago. This prince had read the *Book of Thoth*, whose magic taught people how to speak with animals. Setna longed to learn this ancient wisdom.

Setna went to Prince Neferkeptah's tomb and there, on the prince's mummy, lay the *Book of Thoth*. As Setna reached for the book, the spirit of Prince Neferkeptah's wife spoke to him. She told Setna how the *Book of Thoth* had brought their family bad luck – she had drowned along with her young son. Setna did not heed the warning, and he took the book. In time, Setna was troubled by terrible visions. He dreamt his children were killed and his wife became a beggar. Fearing that his nightmares would come true, Setna returned the *Book of Thoth* to the tomb. He laid it on the mummy of Prince Neferkeptah, where it rests, unread, to this day.

Many different gods were worshipped in ancient Egypt. Major gods, such as Isis and Osiris, were popular all over the country. Minor gods were popular in only a few towns and villages. The spirits of the gods were believed to live in the temples that were built in their honour. The gods were constantly offered gifts and prayers to please them. In return, they looked after Egypt. But if they became angry, disaster would strike.

SEVEN YEARS OF FAMINE

For seven years the river Nile did not flood. The fertile land of Egypt became barren; crops withered and people starved. The pharaoh asked the vizier, his most important official, for advice. He wanted to know where the river's flood began, and which god controlled its swelling waters. The vizier replied that Khnum was the god, and that the river began its flood far to the south.

The pharaoh travelled to that distant place, where he found a temple to the god Khnum. It was deserted and in ruins. People no longer went there – it was as if they had stopped believing in Khnum. The pharaoh entered the temple, prayed to Khnum and had the temple rebuilt. This devotion pleased Khnum and he opened the river's floodgates. Once again, the Nile flooded the land. Crops grew and the famine came to an end. The pharaoh saw it was wrong for people to forget Khnum, so he ordered more temples to be built in the god's name, and prayers to be said.

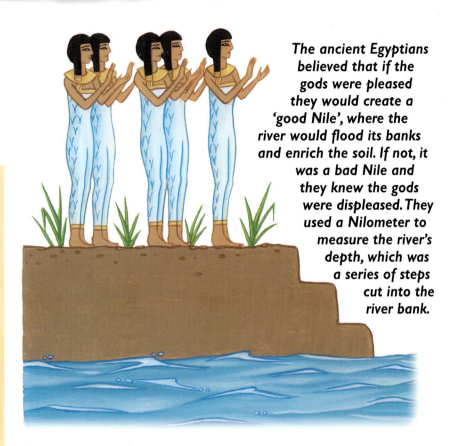

The ancient Egyptians believed that if the gods were pleased they would create a 'good Nile', where the river would flood its banks and enrich the soil. If not, it was a bad Nile and they knew the gods were displeased. They used a Nilometer to measure the river's depth, which was a series of steps cut into the river bank.

The huge temples of Egypt covered vast areas of land and were entered through tall gateways known as pylons. The holiest room in the temple contained a statue of the god, within which he was thought to live.

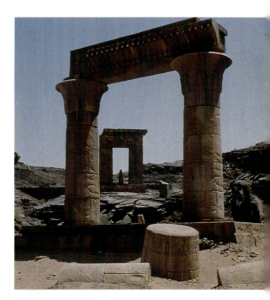

In the film **The Mummy**, Imhotep has slept for over 3,000 years, buried deep beneath the ruined temples. He is disturbed and resurrected when treasure hunters, searching the tombs of the buried pharaohs, discover his resting place.

GLOSSARY

AMMUT
A creature whose body was half lion and half hippopotamus, with the head of a crocodile. It ate the hearts of the dead who were not fit to enter the underworld.

AMULET
A good luck charm used to protect the wearer from harm.

ANUBIS
God of embalming.

APEP
Snake-god of the underworld who represented the forces of chaos and evil.

BARQUE
A boat. The sun-god Ra travelled in a solar barque.

BENU-BIRD
A mysterious bird, rather like the legendary phoenix, which seemed to die then rise again. This is why it was linked with the sun-god Ra.

CANOPIC JARS
Four jars that held the lungs, liver, intestines and stomach of a mummy.

CROOK
A short stick with a curved top. It was part of the royal regalia.

CROWN
There were several designs of crown, worn by the pharaoh as part of the royal regalia.

EMBALM
To preserve a body with perfumes, resins and oils.

FERTILE STRIP
The thin strip of fertile land on either side of the river Nile on which Egyptian civilization flourished.

FLAIL
Three strings of beads on a stick. It was part of the royal regalia.

GEB
God of the earth.

HAPY
God of the Nile's flood.

HATHOR
Goddess of women.

HIEROGLYPHS
The writing of ancient Egypt. Signs recorded the sounds and meaning of words.

HORUS
God of the sky, Kingship, and the keeper of order. Son of Osiris and Isis.

ISIS
Goddess of fertility and nature. Sister and wife of Osiris, and mother of Horus.

KEMET
The ancient Egyptians called their country Kemet (black land) after the mud deposited by the river Nile.

KHEPRI
God of the sun, creation and dawn.

KHNUM
God who made the river Nile flood each year.

LOTUS
A water lily which grew along the banks of the river Nile.

LOWER EGYPT
The low-lying, northern part of Egypt, the Delta.

MUD-BRICK
A building material made from dried mud.

MUMMY
An animal or human body preserved by embalming.

NILOMETER
Steps with a scale to measure the height of the river Nile flood.

NUN
God of the ocean of chaos.

NUT
Goddess of the sky.

OBELISK
A tall, slender stone with a pyramid-shaped top.

OSIRIS
God of the underworld, the dead, and rebirth.

PHARAOH
An Egyptian king.

PRIMEVAL MOUND
The hill that rose out of the waters of Nun. It was the first land.

PTAH
God of creation.

PYLON
The towers flanking the entrance to a temple.

RA
Creator sun-god, usually shown as a man with a hawk's head and a sun-disc headdress.

SCARAB
A species of large beetle. Amulets were often made in the shape of a scarab.

SCRIBE
A person who could read and write.

SEKHMET
Goddess of war and healing.

SELKET
Goddess who protected people from poisonous bites and stings.

SETH
God of chaos, storms, and evil. Brother of Osiris.

SHU
God of the air and sunlight.

SPHINX
A mythical creature with the head of a man, often a pharaoh, and the body of a lion.

THOTH
God of wisdom, writing, reading, mathematics, and magic.

UPPER EGYPT
The southern area of Egypt, the Nile valley.

WEDJAT-EYE
The eye of Horus. It was a symbol of healing and was worn as an amulet.

VIZIER
The highest official in Egypt. He informed the pharaoh about everything that happened and saw that the king's instructions were carried out.

WEIGHING OF THE HEART
A ceremony in which a dead person's heart was weighed against the feather of truth to see if they deserved to enter the afterlife.

INDEX

KINGFISHER/UNIVERSAL
Kingfisher Publications Plc
New Penderel House
283-288 High Holborn
London WC1V 7HZ
www.kingfisherpub.com

First published by Kingfisher
Publications Plc 2002
10 9 8 7 6 5 4 3 2 1

1TR/1201/TWP/MAR(MAR)/130SINAR

Copyright © Kingfisher
Publications Plc 2002

© 2002 Universal Studios Publishing
Rights, a division of Universal Studios
Licensing, Inc. The Mummy and The
Mummy Returns is a trademark and
copyright of Universal Studios.

A CIP catalogue record for this
book is available from the British
Library.

ISBN 0 7534 0742 6

Printed in Singapore